# LOUDMOUTH GEORGE EARNS HIS ALLOWANCE

# Nancy Carlson

 CAROLRHODA BOOKS, INC. MINNEAPOLIS · NEW YORK

In honor of Mik's graduation!  GOOD JOB!!
Now could you please put your clothes away?
 MOM

Text and illustrations copyright © 2007 by Nancy Carlson

Carolrhoda Books, Inc.
A division of Lerner Publishing Group
241 First Avenue North
Minneapolis, MN 55401  U.S.A.

Website address: www.lernerbooks.com


Library of Congress Cataloging-in-Publication Data

Carlson, Nancy L.
    Loudmouth George earns his allowance / by Nancy Carlson.
       p. cm.
    Summary: George tries to trick his brothers into doing his chores for him so that he can go to the movies with his friend, but things do not turn out exactly the way he wants them to.
    ISBN-13: 978−0−8225−6560−4 (lib. bdg. : alk. paper)
    ISBN-10: 0−8225−6560−9 (lib. bdg. : alk. paper)   [1. Work—Fiction.  2. Brothers—Fiction.  3. Rabbits—Fiction.]   I. Title.
PZ7.C21665Lr 2007
[E]—dc22                                                                                             2006013840

Manufactured in the United States of America
1 2 3 4 5 6 − JR − 12 11 10 09 08 07

| | George | TONY | Danny | LARS | TiM |
|---|---|---|---|---|---|
| M | clean room | put crayons away | clean room | set table | pick up Toys |
| T | Dust living Room | Dry dishes | put recycling out | put out Garbage | make Bed |
| W | Sweep Garage | pick up Room | Get mail | put dishes Away | put Dirty towels in WASH |
| Th | Weed Garden | Clean counters | flatten soda cans | Get Mail | Dust Bed-room |
| F | Fill Feeders | pick up Toys | sweep the walk | put games Away | Get Mail |

It was summer vacation, and George's mom gave him a chore to do each day.

But on Monday, George was too busy playing video games to clean his room.

On Tuesday, he was too busy building his fort to dust the living room.

On Wednesday, George was too busy watching TV to sweep the garage.

On Thursday, he was too busy swimming to weed the garden.

On Friday, George was supposed to fill the bird feeders.
But Harriet called to invite him to the movies.

When George asked his mom for his allowance, she said, "No allowance for the movies until you do your chores. And while I'm at the store, please watch your little brothers."

After his mother left, George thought of a great idea.
"I'll get my brothers to do my chores!"

"Hey, guys.  If you do my chores, I'll take
you to the movies with me!"
"Oh boy!" said his brothers.

So Lars got busy cleaning George's room, and Tim got busy dusting the living room.

Danny got busy sweeping
the garage, and Tony got
busy weeding the garden.

"Boy, are my brothers suckers! After doing all of my chores, they'll be way too tired to go to the movies!" laughed George.

George was just about to relax when Mikey asked, "What should I do?" "You can fill those feeders," said George.

But Mikey
climbed to the
top of the tree
and got stuck!

So George had to climb way up high and
help him down.

As George was filling the feeders, Danny said, "Oops! I spilled a little paint in the garage."

So George had to clean up the paint AND
sweep the garage.

When George was finished,
Tim said, "I'm all done dusting."

"Oh no!" said George.  "The living room is a mess!"

So George had to finish the dusting AND
clean up the living room.

Just as George finished
dusting, Tony said,
"Look! I pulled out all the weeds!"
"Oh no!" cried George. "Those
aren't weeds. They're flowers!"

So George had to replant the flowers AND
pull out the weeds.

After George was done
weeding, Lars said,
"Your room is all clean."

But when George saw his room, he said,
"It's worse than before!"

While George cleaned up his room, his brothers
made a mess in the kitchen and . . .

Mikey found a chocolate bar.

So George had to clean the kitchen AND

give Mikey a bath!

When George was finally finished, his mother came home and said, "I see all of your chores are done, and you even gave Mikey a bath!"

Then she reached into her purse and said, "Good job, George! Here's your allowance for the movies."

When Harriet came to pick him up for the
movies, George said, "I'm way too tired to go!"

But his brothers said,
"We're not."

And off they went to the movies while . . .

George took a
**l-o-o-o-n g**
nap!